OUR Columbus Day BOOK

by Jane Belk Moncure
illustrated by Jean Shackelford

THE CHILD'S WORLD

ELGIN, ILLINOIS 60120

Distributed by Childrens Press, 1224 West Van Buren Street, Chicago, Illinois 60607.

Library of Congress Cataloging in Publication Data

Moncure, Jane Belk.
  Our Columbus Day book.

  (A Special-day book)
  Summary: Describes a class' activities
to prepare for Columbus Day.
  1. Columbus Day—Juvenile literature. 2. Columbus,
Christopher—Juvenile literature. 3. America—Discovery
and exploration-Spanish-Juvenile literature.
[1. Columbus Day] I. Shackelford, Jean, ill. II. Title.
III. Series.
E120.M74 1986   970.01'5   86-6818
ISBN 0-89565-347-8

1 2 3 4 5 6 7 8 9 10 11 12 R 95 94 93 92 91 90 89 88 87 86

OUR Columbus Day BOOK

This book is about how we celebrated Columbus Day in our class. You will have more ideas in your class.

On Columbus Day we found a big suitcase in the middle of the rug.

"Where are we going today?" Lisa asked.

"Come and sit by the suitcase, and I will tell you," Miss Taylor said.

5

She opened her suitcase and took
out some pictures. "We are going to
take a story trip with Christopher
Columbus," she said. "He lived long
ago.

"If you had gone on a trip over land
back then, you would have traveled
by camel or horse or elephant."

"Wow!" said Carl. "That would
have been fun."

"On the ocean, people traveled in sailing ships," said Miss Taylor.

"What made the ships move?" asked Carl.

"The wind blew on the sails. It pushed the ships through the water." Miss Taylor gave Joe a little boat with a sail. Then she poured some water in a pan.

"What happens when you blow on the ship?" Miss Taylor asked.

"It moves!" said Joe.

"Just like the ships moved when the wind blew," said Carl.

Then Miss Taylor showed us a globe. "This is a model of our world," she said.

"This is America. We live here. Long ago, people on the other side of the ocean did not know that our land was here."

Miss Taylor turned the globe. "This

is the land on the other side of the ocean," she said. "This is Europe. Christopher Columbus lived here. As I turn the globe, you will see much more land. It is called Asia. People traveled for months to cross this land. They wanted to buy gold and pearls and something special from the Spice Islands of the Indies.

She took some spice boxes out of her suitcase. "They bought spices like these," she said.

"You can smell these spices. Even today, many spices come from the Spice Islands."

"They smell so good!" said Lisa.

"Spicy," said Rolanda.

"Back then, people needed spices to make their food taste good," Miss Taylor said. "So it was important to travel to the Spice Islands.

"But in times of war, it was hard to get there by land. So someone needed to find another way."

Miss Taylor showed us a picture of Christopher Columbus.

"Columbus was a great sailor. He thought the world was round," she said. "He thought he could get to India by going just the opposite of the way others went. He thought he could get there by sailing across the ocean.

"He needed ships, sailors, supplies, and money. He asked many rich and powerful people for help.

"Finally, after years of waiting, the king and queen of Spain helped Columbus."

"I would have said 'yes' to Columbus," said Joe.

"Me, too," said Sue.

Miss Taylor gave crowns to Joe and
Sue, so they could be king and queen
of Spain. The rest of us were Columbus and his sailors.

"The king and queen of Spain gave Columbus three ships. They were the *Niña*, the *Pinta*, and the *Santa Maria*."

"If I had been there long ago, I would have sailed with Columbus," said Carl.

"Me, too," said Rolanda.

"Here is a list of some food you would have taken on such a long trip," said Miss Taylor.

"I only like raisins!" said Carl.

Miss Taylor gave all her "sailors" raisins to taste. Then she pulled a big map from her suitcase.

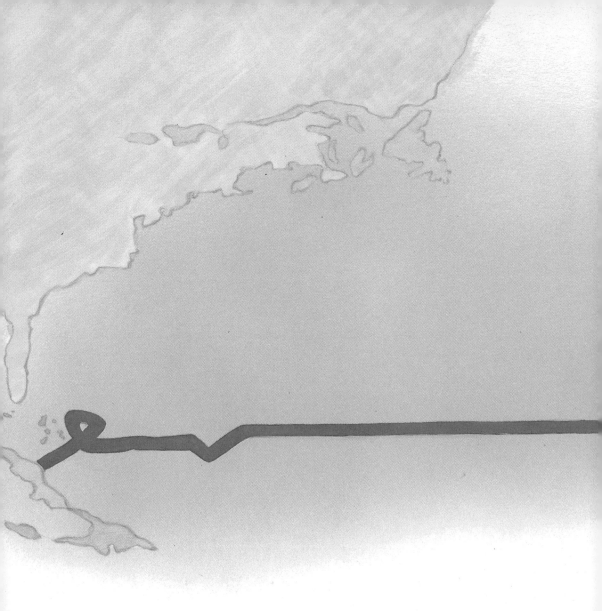

"This is how Columbus sailed across the ocean," she said. "Early in the morning on August 3, 1492, his three little ships sailed out of their home harbor.

"Soon they headed west—across the unknown sea.

"Many times the sailors wanted to turn around. But Columbus would not go back. He said, 'Sail On!' "

"I would have kept going too," said Carl.

"They sailed for weeks. Finally. . . at long last, Columbus believed land was near. First, he saw a bird. . .then many birds. . .then a green branch came floating by in the water. It had a flower on it.

"Someone saw a crab floating. And there was fresh green seaweed.

"Columbus was sure land was near.

"And it was. Very early in the morning on October 12, 1492, someone shouted, 'Land! Land ahead!'

"There, in the moonlight, Columbus saw land.

"Columbus led his sailors ashore. They said a prayer of thanks. They were safe on land.

"Columbus thought he was in India.
But he wasn't. He had really come to
a new land. He had come to the
part of the world that we know as
America.

"When Columbus saw the friendly people in the new land, he called them Indians. Columbus gave them red wool caps, glass beads, and tiny brass bells.

"They gave him parrots and balls of cotton.

"Columbus didn't get to India, but he found a rich New World. And later, because of him, other sailors did find a new way to the Spice Islands."

Miss Taylor showed us many things
Columbus found in the New World.
One of the things was corn.

"Later, people learned they could pop some of the Indian corn," she told us.

We popped some corn.

"Mmm, smells good!" said Joe.

"When Columbus went home,"
Miss Taylor said, "the king and queen
gave him a royal welcome. Everyone
wanted to hear about his great
discovery.

"Columbus took some Indian friends
back to Spain to meet the king and
queen. And he took flowers, plants,
and a sweet-tasting fruit. We call it
pineapple."

Miss Taylor took a pineapple out of
her suitcase. "Now we can taste a
pineapple," she said, "just as Columbus may have tasted one long ago."

"I'm glad Columbus found America,"
said Carl.

"We are all glad," said Miss Taylor.
"That's why we have Columbus Day."